For Weenie, who reminds me daily that good things
come in small packages
S.W.

For Rob, Kym, Maria Mehera, Shauna, and Alexandra
W.L.

uP↑

Happy
Birthday, Frankie
Text copyright © 1999 by Sarah
Weeks Illustrations copyright © 1999 by Warren Linn
Printed in the U.S.A. All rights reserved. http://www.harperchildrens.com
Library of Congress Cataloging-in-Publication Data   Weeks, Sarah. Happy Birthday, Frankie
/ by Sarah Weeks ; illustrated by Warren Linn.   p.   cm.   "A Laura Geringer book."
Summary: A professor tries to assemble Frankenstein's body parts so that the
monster can enjoy his birthday cake, with unexpected results.
ISBN 0-06-027965-6. — ISBN 0-06-028522-2 (lib. bdg.)
[1. Monsters—Fiction.   2. Birthdays—Fiction.   3. Humorous stories.]   I.
Linn, Warren, ill.   II. Title. PZ7.W42235Hap 1999 98-52966 [E]—dc21 CIP   AC
Typography by Alicia Mikles 1 2 3 4 5 6 7 8 9 10
First Edition

Happy birthday, Frankie

BY SARAH WEEKS   ILLUSTRATED BY WARREN LINN

DISCARDED

UP ↑

A LAURA GERINGER BOOK
AN IMPRINT OF HARPERCOLLINS PUBLISHERS

Hm_m_m_m…

CONTAINS SMALL PARTS.
Screw (A) to (B)· to (C)
ELBOW hinges (M1)
BATTERIES NOT
INCLUDED.

The
leg bone's
connected
to the...

Oh, dear.

The
arm bone's

connected to the . . .

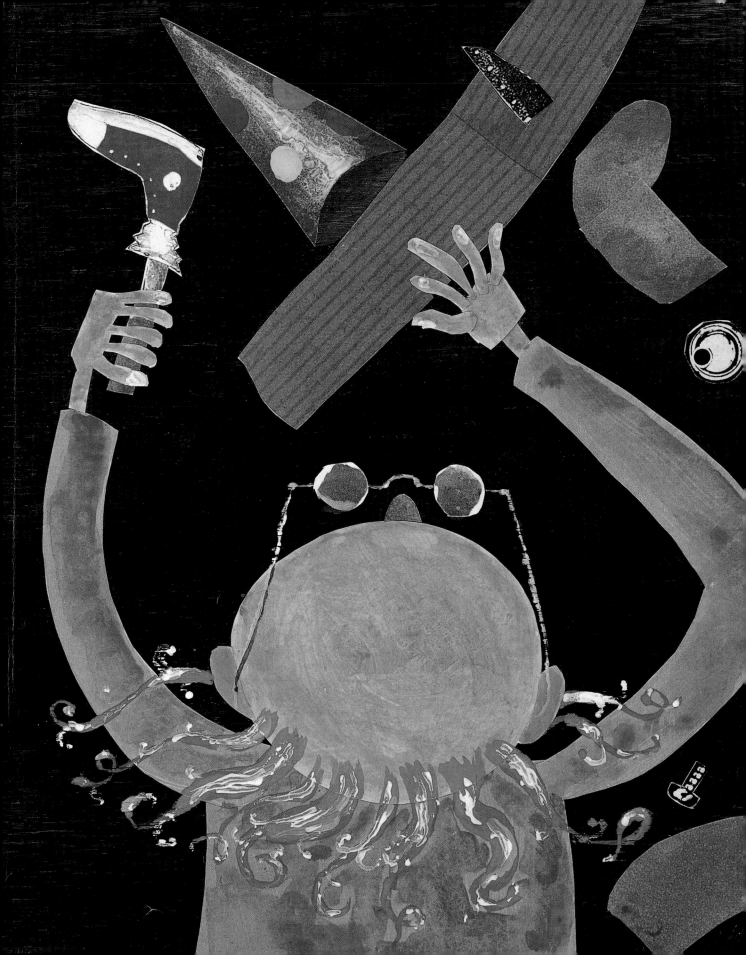

Nope.

Aha!

WHOOPS.

The
foot bone's

connected
to the...

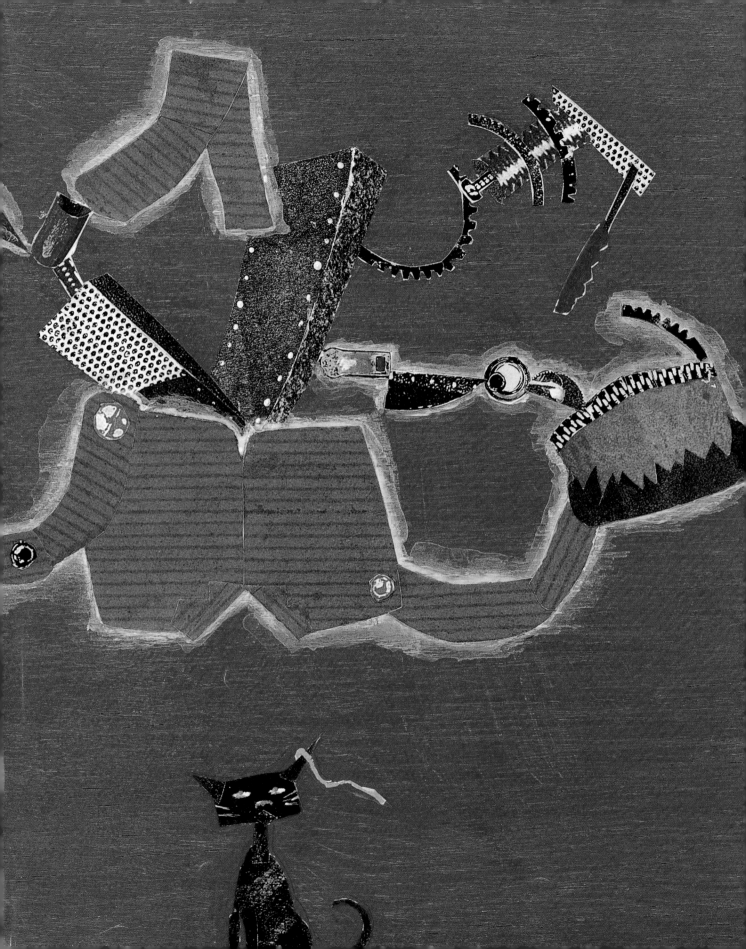

The neck bone's

connected
to the . . .

Yes!

Happy Birthday, Frankie!

Blow out
the candle . . .

Hmmmm...

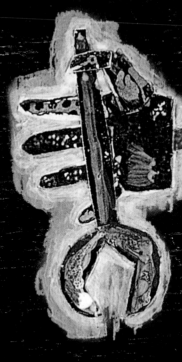

The leg bone's connected to the . . . .